STANLEY'S
Christmas Adventure

JEFF BROWN

STANLEY'S
Christmas Adventure

Illustrated by Philippe Dupasquier

MAMMOTH

For Duncan

First published in Great Britain 1993
by Methuen Children's Books Ltd
Published 1994 by Mammoth
an imprint of Reed Consumer Books Ltd
Michelin House, 81 Fulham Road, London SW3 6RB
and Auckland, Melbourne, Singapore and Toronto

Reprinted 1994

Text copyright © 1993 Jeff Brown
Illustrations copyright © 1993 Philippe Dupasquier

The right of Jeff Brown to be identified as author of this
work has been asserted by him in accordance with
the Copyright, Designs and Patents Act 1988

ISBN 0 7497 1820 X

A CIP catalogue record for this title
is available from the British Library

Printed and bound in Great Britain
by Cox & Wyman Ltd, Reading, Berkshire

Contents

PROLOGUE

She was the sort of little girl who liked to be *sure* of things, so she went all over Snow City, checking up.

The elves had done their work.

At the Post Office, Mail Elves had read the letters, making lists of who wanted what.

In the great workshops – the Doll Room, the Toy Plant, thc Game Mill – Gift Elves had filled the orders, taking care as to colour and size and style.

In the Wrap Shed the gifts lay ready, wrapped now in gay paper with holly and pine cones, sorted by country, by city or village, by road or lane or street.

The Wrap Elves teased her. 'Don't trust us, eh? . . . Snooping, we call this, Miss!'

'Pooh!' said the little girl. 'Well done, elves! Good work!'

But at home in Snow City Square, all was not well.

'Don't slam the door, dear,' said her mother, weeping. 'Your father's having his nap.'

'Mother! What's wrong?'

'He won't go this year, he says!' The mother sobbed. 'He's been so cross lately, but I never – '

'*Why? Why* won't he go?'

'They've lost faith, don't care any more, he says! Surely not *everyone*, I said. Think of your favourite letter, the one by your desk! He just growled at me!'

'Pooh!' said the girl. 'It's not fair! Really! I mean, everything's *ready*! Why – '

'Not now, dear,' said the mother. 'It's been a dreadful day.'

In the little office at the back of the house, the girl studied the letter her mother had mentioned, framed with others on a wall:

I am a regular boy, except that I got flat, the letter said. *From an accident. I was going to ask for new clothes, but my mother already bought them. She had to, because of the flatness. So I'm just writing to say don't bother about me. Have a*

8

nice holiday. My father says be careful driving, there are lots of bad drivers this time of year.

The girl thought for a moment, and an idea came to her. 'Hmmmm . . . Well, why *not*?' she said.

She looked again at the letter.

The name LAMBCHOP was printed across the top, and an address. It was signed 'Stanley, U.S.A.'

CHAPTER ONE

Sarah

It was two nights before Christmas, and all through the house not a Lambchop was stirring, but something was.

Stanley Lambchop sat up in his bed. 'Listen! Someone said "Rat."'

'It was more like "grat,"' said his younger brother Arthur, from his bed. 'In the living room, I think.'

The brothers tiptoed down the stairs.

For a moment all was silence in the darkened living room. Then came a *thump*. 'Ouch!' said a small voice. 'Drat again!'

'Are you a burglar?' Arthur called. 'Did you hurt yourself?'

10

'I am *not* a burglar!' said the voice. 'Where's the – Ah!' The lights came on.

The brothers stared.

Before the fireplace, by the Christmas tree, stood a slender, dark-haired little girl wearing a red jacket and skirt, both trimmed with white fur.

'I banged it *twice*,' she said, rubbing her knee. 'Coming down the chimney, and just now.'

'We *do* have a front door, you know,' said Stanley.

'Well, so does my house. But, you know, this time of year . . .?' The girl sounded a bit nervous. 'Actually, I've never done this before. Let's see . . . Ha, ha, ha! Season's Greetings! Ha, ha, ha!

'"Ha, ha!" to you,' said Arthur. 'What's so funny?'

'Funny?' said the girl. 'Oh! "Ho, ho, ho!" I meant. I'm Sarah Christmas. Who are you?'

'Arthur Lambchop,' said Arthur. 'That's my brother Stanley.'

'It is? But he's not *flat*.'

'He was, but I blew him up,' Arthur explained. 'With a bicycle pump.'

'Oh, no! I wish you hadn't.' Sarah Christmas sank into a chair. 'Drat! It's all going wrong! Perhaps I shouldn't have come. But that's how

11

I am. Headstrong, my mother says. She – '

'Excuse me,' Stanley said. 'But where are you from?'

'And why *did* you come?' said Arthur.

Sarah told them.

Mr and Mrs Lambchop were reading in bed.

A tap came at the door, and then Stanley's voice. 'Hey! Can I come in?'

Mr and Mrs Lambchop cared greatly for proper speech. 'Hay is for horses, Stanley,' she said. 'And not "can" dear. You *may* come in.'

Stanley came in.

'What is the explanation, my boy, of this late call?' said Mr Lambchop, remembering past surprises. 'You have not, I see, become flat again. Has a genie come to visit? Or perhaps the President of the United States has called?'

Mrs Lambchop smiled. 'You are very amusing, George.'

'Arthur and I were in bed,' said Stanley. 'But we heard a noise and went to see. It was a girl called Sarah Christmas, from Snow City. She talks a lot. She says her father says he won't come this year, but Sarah thinks he might change his mind if I ask him to. Because I wrote him a letter once that he liked. She wants me to go with her to Snow City. In her father's sleigh.

It's at the North Pole, I think.' Stanley caught his breath. 'I said I'd have to ask you first.'

'Quite right,' said Mrs Lambchop.

Mr Lambchop went to the bathroom and drank a glass of water to calm himself.

'Now then, Stanley,' he said, returning. 'You have greatly startled us. Surely – '

'Put on your robe, George,' said Mrs Lambchop. 'Let us hear for ourselves what this visitor has to say.'

'This is *delicious*!' Sarah Christmas sipped the hot chocolate Mrs Lambchop had served them all. 'My mother makes it too, with cinnamon in it. And little cookies with – ' Her glance had fallen on the mantelpiece. 'What's *that*, pinned up there?'

'Christmas stockings,' Stanley said. 'The blue one's mine.'

'But the other, the great square thing?'

'It's a pillow case.' Arthur blushed. 'My stocking wouldn't do. I have very small feet.'

'Pooh!' Sarah laughed. 'You wanted extra gifts, so – '

'Sarah, dear,' Mrs Lambchop said. 'Your father? Has he truly made up his mind, you think?'

'Oh, yes!' Sarah sighed. 'But I thought – Stanley being flat, that *really* interested him. I mean, I couldn't be *sure*, but if nobody ever did anything without – '

'You seem a very nice girl, Sarah.' Mr Lambchop gave a little laugh. 'But you *have* been joking with us, surely? I – '

The phone rang, and he answered it.

'Hello, George,' the caller said. 'This is your neighbour, Frank Smith. I know it's late, but I

must congratulate you on your Christmas lawn display! Best – '

'Lawn?' said Mr Lambchop. 'Display?'

'The sleigh! And those life-like *reindeer*! What makes them move about like that? Batteries, I suppose?'

'Just a moment, Frank.' Mr Lambchop went

to the window and looked out, Mrs Lambchop beside him.

'My goodness!' she said. 'One, two, three, four . . . Eight! And such a pretty sleigh!'

Mr Lambchop returned to the phone. 'They *are* life-like, aren't they? Goodbye. Thank you for calling, Frank.'

'See? I'm not a joking kind of person, actually,' said Sarah Christmas. 'Now! My idea *might* work, even without the flatness. Do let Stanley go!'

'To the North Pole?' said Mrs Lambchop. 'At night? By himself? Good gracious, Sarah!'

'It's not fair, asking Stanley, but not me,' said Arthur, feeling hurt. 'It's always like this! I never – '

'Oh, pooh!' Sarah Christmas smiled. 'Actually . . . You could *all* go. It's a very big sleigh.'

Mr and Mrs Lambchop looked at each other, then at Stanley and Arthur, then at each other again.

'Stanley just might make a difference, George,' Mrs Lambchop said. 'And if we can *all* go . . .?'

'Quite right,' said Mr Lambchop. 'Sarah, we will accompany you to Snow City!'

'Hooray!' shouted Stanley and Arthur, and

17

Sarah too.

Mrs Lambchop thought they should wait until Frank Smith had gone to bed. 'Imagine the gossip,' she said, 'were he to see our reindeer fly away.'

Mr Lambchop called his office to leave a message on the night-time answering machine. He would not be in tomorrow, he said, as he had been called unexpectedly out of town.

'There!' cried Stanley, by the window. 'The Smiths' light is out.'

The Lambchops changed quickly from pyjamas to warmer clothing, and followed Sarah to the sleigh.

CHAPTER TWO

The Sleigh

'Welcome aboard!' said Sarah, from the driver's seat.

The Lambchops, sitting on little benches that made the big sleigh resemble a roofless bus, could scarcely contain their excitement.

The night sky shone bright with stars, and from the windows of nearby houses red and green Christmas lights twinkled over snowy lawns and streets. Before them, the eight reindeer, fur shiny in the moonlight, tossed their antlered heads.

'Ready when you are, Sarah,' Mr Lambchop said.

'Good!' Sarah cleared her throat. 'Fasten your

seat belts, please! We are about to depart for Snow City. My name is Sarah – I guess you know that – and I'll be glad to answer any questions you may have. Please do not move about without permission of the Sleigh Master – that's me, at least right now – and obey whatever instructions may – '

'Pu-leeese!' said Arthur.

'Oh, all right!' The Lambchops fastened their seat belts, and Sarah took up the reins. 'Ready, One? Ready, Two, Three – '

'Just *numbers*?' cried Mrs Lambchop. 'Why, we know such lovely reindeer names! Dasher, Dancer, Prancer, Vixen – '

'Comet, Cupid, Donder, Blitzen!' shouted Arthur. 'They're from a poem we know!'

'Those *are* good names!' said Sarah. 'Ready, One through Eight?'

The reindeer pawed the ground, jingling their harness bells.

'Now!' said Sarah.

The jingling stopped suddenly, and a great silence fell.

Now a silver mist rose, swirling, about the sleigh. The startled Lambchops could see nothing beyond the mist, not their house nor the houses of their neighbours, not the twinkling Christmas lights, not the bright stars above. There was only the silver mist, everywhere, cool against their cheeks.

'What is this, Sarah?' Mrs Lambchop called. 'Are we not to proceed to Snow City?'

Sarah's voice came cheerfully through the mist. 'We have proceeded. We're there!'

CHAPTER THREE

Snow City

Beyond the mist, excited voices rose. 'Sarah's back! . . . With strangers! Big ones! . . . Where's she been?'

'Poppa's elves,' said Sarah's voice. As she spoke, the mist swirled, then vanished as suddenly as it had come. Above them, the stars shone bright again.

The sleigh rested now in a snow-covered square, in front of a pretty red-roofed house. All about the square were tiny cottages, their windows aglow with light.

Elves surrounded the sleigh. 'Who *are* these people? . . . Is it true, what we've heard? . . . Ask Sarah! She'll know!'

24

The Lambchops smiled and waved. The elves seemed much like ordinary men and women, except that they had pointy ears, very wrinkled faces, and were only about half as tall as Arthur. All wore leather breeches or skirts with wide pockets from which tools and needles stuck out.

'Miss Sarah!' came a voice. 'Is it true? He won't go this year?'

Sarah hesitated. 'Well, sort of . . . But perhaps the Lambchops here . . . Be patient. Go home, please!'

The elves straggled off toward their cottages, grumbling. 'Not going? . . . Hah! After all our work? . . . The *Who*chops? . . . I'd go work somewhere else, but *where?*'

A plump lady in an apron bustled out of the red-roofed house. 'Sarah! Are you all right? Going off like that! Though we did find your note. Gracious! Are those *all* Lambchops, dear?'

'I'm fine, Momma!' said Sarah. 'They wouldn't let Stanley come by himself. That's Stanley, there. The other one's Arthur. Stanley *was* flat, but he got round again.'

'Clever!' said Mrs Christmas. 'Well! Do all come in! Are you fond of hot chocolate?'

' . . . an excellent plan, I do see that. But – Oh, he's in *such* a state! And with Stanley no longer flat . . .' Mrs Christmas sighed. 'More chocolate, Lambchops? I add a dash of cinnamon. Tasty, yes?

'Delicious,' said Mrs Lambchop.

Everyone sat silent, sipping.

Mr Lambchop felt the time had come. 'May

we see him now, Mrs Christmas? We should be getting home. So much to do, this time of year.'

'You forget where you are, George,' said Mrs Lambchop. 'Mrs Christmas, surely, is aware of the demands of the season.'

'I'm sorry about not being flat,' Stanley said.

'I did get tired of it, though.'

'No need to apologise,' said Mrs Christmas. 'Flat, round, whatever, people must be what shape they wish.'

'So true,' said Mrs Lambchop. 'But will your husband agree?'

'We shall see. Come.' Mrs Christmas rose, and the Lambchops followed her down the hall.

Mrs Christmas knocked on a door. 'Visitors, dear! From America.'

'Send 'em back!' said a deep voice.

'Sir?' Mr Lambchop tried to sound cheerful. 'A few minutes, perhaps? "'Tis the season to be jolly", eh? We –'

'Bah!' said the voice. 'Go home!'

'What a terrible temper!' Stanley said. 'He doesn't want to meet us at all!'

'I already *have* met him once,' Arthur whispered. 'In a department store.'

'That wasn't the real one, dear,' Mrs Lambchop said.

'Too bad,' said Arthur. 'He was much nicer than this one.'

Sarah stepped forward. 'Poppa? Can you hear me, Poppa?'

'I hear you, all right!' said the deep voice. 'Took the Great Sleigh without permission, didn't you? Rascal!'

'The letter on your wall, Poppa?' Sarah said. 'The Lambchop letter? Well, they're *here*, the whole family! It wasn't easy, Poppa! I went down their chimney and scraped my knee, and then I banged it, the *same* knee, when I –'

'SARAH!' said the voice.

Sarah hushed, and so did everyone else.

'The flat boy, eh?' said the voice. 'Hmmmm . . .'

Mrs Lambchop took a comb from her bag and tidied Arthur's hair. Mr Lambchop straightened Stanley's collar.

'Come in!' said the voice behind the door.

CHAPTER FOUR

Sarah's Father

The room was very dark, but it was possible to make out a desk at the far side, and someone seated behind it.

The Lambchops held their breaths. This was perhaps the most famous person in the world!

'Guess what, Poppa?' said Sarah, sounding quite nervous. 'The Lambchops know *names* for our reindeer!'

No answer came.

'Names, Poppa, not just *numbers*! There's Dashes and Frances and –'

'Dasher,' said Stanley, 'Then Dancer, then –'

'*Then* Frances! cried Sarah. 'Or is it *Prances*? Then –'

'Waste of time, this!' said the figure behind
the desk. But then a switch clicked, and lights
came on.

The Lambchops stared.

Except for a large TV in one corner and a
speaker-box on the desk, the room was much

like Mr Lambchop's study at home. There were bookshelves and comfortable chairs. Framed letters, one of them Stanley's, hung behind the desk, along with photographs of Mrs Christmas, Sarah, and elves and reindeer, singly and in groups.

Sarah's father was large and stout, but otherwise not what they had expected.

He wore a blue zip jacket with 'N. Pole Athletic Club' lettered across it, and sat with his feet, in fuzzy brown slippers, up on the desk. His long white hair and beard were in need of trimming, and the beard had crumbs in it. On the desk, along with his feet, were a plate of cookies, a bowl of potato chips, and a bottle of strawberry soda with a straw in it.

'George Lambchop, sir,' said Mr Lambchop. 'Good evening. May I present my wife Harriet, and our sons Stanley and Arthur?'

'How do you do.' Sarah's father sipped his soda. 'Whichever is Stanley, step forward, please, and turn about.'

Stanley stepped forward and turned about.

'You're *round*, boy!'

'I blew him up,' said Arthur. 'With a bicycle pump.'

Sarah's father raised his eyebrows. 'Very funny. Very funny indeed.' He ate some potato chips. 'Well? What brings you all here?'

Mr Lambchop cleared his throat. 'I understand, Mr – No, that can't be right. What *is* the proper form of address?'

'Depends where you're from. 'Santa' is the American way. But I'm known also as Father

34

Christmas, *Père Noel, Babbo Natale, Julenisse* . . . Little country, way off somewhere, they call me "The Great Hugga Wagoo."'

'Hugga Wagoo?' Arthur laughed loudly, and Mrs Lambchop shook her head at him.

Mr Lambchop continued. 'We understand, sir – *Santa*, if I may? – that you propose not to make your rounds this year. We are here to ask that you reconsider.'

'Reconsider?' said Sarah's father. 'The way things are these days? Hah! See for yourselves!'

The big TV in the corner clicked on, and he switched from channel to channel.

The first channel showed battleships firing flaming missiles; the second, aeroplanes dropping bombs; the third, cars crashing other cars. Then came buildings burning, people begging for food, people hitting each other, people firing pistols at policemen. The last channel showed a game show, men and women in chicken costumes grabbing for prizes in a pool of mud.

Sarah's father switched off the TV. 'Peace on Earth? Goodwill toward men? Been wasting my time, it seems!'

'You have been watching *far* too much television,' said Mrs Lambchop. 'No wonder

you take a dim view of things.'

'Facts are facts, madam! Everywhere, violence and greed! Hah! Right here in my own office, a whole family come begging for Christmas treats!'

The Lambchops were deeply shocked.

'I'm greedy sometimes,' said Stanley. 'But not always.'

'I'm quite nice, actually,' Arthur said. 'And Stanley's even nicer than me.'

'*I*, dear,' said Mrs Lambchop. 'Nicer than *I*.'

Mr Lambchop, finding it hard to believe that he was at the North Pole having a conversation like this, chose his words with care.

'You misjudge us, sir,' he said. 'There is indeed much violence in the world, and selfishness. But not everyone – we Lambchops, for example – '

'Hah! Different, are you?' Sarah's father spoke into the little box on his desk. 'Yo! Elf Ewald?'

'Central Files,' said a voice from the box. 'Ewald here.'

'Ewald,' said Sarah's father 'Check this year's letters, under "U.S.A." Bring me the "Lambchop" file.'

CHAPTER FIVE

The Letters

Elf Ewald had come and gone, leaving behind a large brown folder.

'Not greedy, Lambchops? We shall see!' Sarah's father drew a letter from the folder and read it aloud.

' "Dear Santa, My parents say I can't have a real car until I'm grown up. I want one now. A big red one. Make that two cars, both red." Hah! Hear that? Shameful!'

Mrs Lambchop shook her head. 'I should be interested,' she said, 'to learn who wrote that letter?'

'It is signed – Hmmmm . . . Frederic. Frederic Lampop.'

Stanley laughed. 'Our name's not "Lampop!" And we don't even know any Frederics!'

'Mistakes *do* happen, you know! I get *millions* of letters!' Sarah's father drew from the folder again. 'Ah! This one's from *you*!'

'"Dear Santa,"' he read. '"I hope you are fine. I need lots of gifts this year. Shoes and socks and shirts and pants and underwear. And big tents. At least a hundred of each would be nice – "' A hundred! *There's* greediness!'

'It does seem a bit much, Stanley,' said Mr Lambchop. 'And why tents, for goodness sake?'

'You'll see,' said Stanley.

Sarah's father read on. '" . . . of each would be nice. But not delivered to my house. It was on TV about a terrible earthquake in South America where all the houses fell down, and people lost all their clothes and don't have anywhere to live. Please take everything to where the earthquake was. Thank you. Your friend, Stanley Lambchop. P.S. I would send my old clothes, but they are mostly from when I was flat and wouldn't fit anybody else."'

'Good for you, Stanley!' said Mrs Lambchop. 'A fine idea, the tents.'

'Hmmph! One letter, that's all.' Sarah's father chose another letter. 'This one's got jam on it.'

'Excuse me,' said Arthur. 'I was eating a

sandwich.'

'"Dear Santa,"' Sarah's father read, '"I have hung up a pillow case instead of a stocking – "' Hah! The old pillow case trick!'

'Wait!' cried Arthur. 'Read the rest!'

'" . . . instead of a stocking. Please fill this up with chocolate bars, my favourite kind with nuts. My brother Stanley is writing to you about an earthquake, and how people there need clothes and tents and things. Well, I think they need food too, and little stoves to cook on. So

40

please give them the chocolate bars, and food and stoves. The bars should be the big kind. It doesn't matter about the nuts. Sincerely, Arthur Lambchop."'

Mrs Lambchop gave Arthur a little hug.

'All right, *two* letters,' said Sarah's father. 'But from brothers. Count as one, really.'

He took a last letter from the folder. 'Nice penmanship, this one . . . Mr and Mrs George Lambchop! Now there's a surprise!'

'Well, why *not*?' said Mrs Lambchop.

Mr Lambchop said, 'No harm, eh, just dropping a line?'

Their letter was read.

'"Dear Sir: Perhaps you expect letters from children only, since as people grow older they often begin to doubt that you truly exist. But when our two sons were very small, and asked if you were real, we said "yes". And if they were to ask again now, we would not say "no". We would say that you are not real, of course, for those who do not believe in you, but very real indeed for those who *do*. Our Christmas wish is that you will never have cause to doubt that Stanley and Arthur Lambchop, and their parents, take the latter position. Sincerely, Mr and Mrs George Lambchop, U.S.A."'

Sarah's father thought for a moment.

41

'Hmmm . . . *Latter* position? Ah! *Do* believe. I see.'

'See, Poppa?' said Sarah. 'No greediness! Not one –'

'Fine letters, Sarah. I agree.' There was sadness in the deep voice now. 'But all, Sarah, from the same family that thought to deceive me with that "flatness" story. Flat indeed!'

Mrs Lambchop gasped. 'Deceive? Oh, no!'

'Round is round, madam.' Sarah's father shook his head. 'The lad's shape speaks for itself.'

The hearts of all the Lambchops sank within them. Their mission had failed, they thought. For millions and millions of children all over the world, a joyful holiday was lost, perhaps never to come again.

Arthur felt especially bad. It was his fault, he told himself, for thinking of that bicycle pump.

Stanley felt worst of all. If only he hadn't grown tired of being flat, hadn't let Arthur blow him round again! If only there were proof –

And then he remembered something.

'Wait!' he shouted, and stood on tiptoe to whisper in Mrs Lambchop's ear.

'What . . .?' she said. 'I can't – The *what*? Oh! Yes! I had forgotten! Good for you, Stanley!'

Rummaging in her bag, she found her wallet,

from which she drew a photograph. She gave it to Sarah's father.

'Do keep that,' she said. 'We have more at home.'

The snapshot had been taken by Mr Lambchop the day after the big bulletin board fell on Stanley. It showed him, quite flat, sliding under a closed door. Only his top half was visible, smiling up at the camera. The bottom half was still behind the door.

For a long moment, as Sarah's father studied the picture, no one spoke.

'My apologies, Lambchops,' he said at last. 'Flat he is. *Was*, anyhow. I've half a mind to – ' He sighed. 'But those red cars, asking for *two*, that – '

'That was Lamb*POP*!' cried Arthur. 'Not –'

'Just teasing, lad!'

Sarah's father had jumped up, a great smile on his face.

'Yo, elves!' he shouted into his speaker phone. 'Prepare to load gifts! Look lively! Tomorrow is Christmas Eve, you know!'

The next moments were joyful indeed.

'Thank you, thank you! . . . Hooray! . . . Hooray! . . . Hooray!' shouted Mr and Mrs Lambchop, and Stanley and Arthur and Sarah.

Sarah's mother kissed everyone. Mrs

Lambchop kissed Sarah's father, and almost fainted when she realized what she had done.

Then Sarah's father asked Stanley to autograph the sliding-under-the-door picture, and when Stanley had written 'All best wishes, S. Lambchop' across the picture, he pinned it to the wall.

'Blew him round, eh?' he said to Arthur. 'Like to have seen that!'

He turned to Sarah. 'Come, my dear! While I freshen up, teach me those reindeer names. Then I will see our visitors safely home!'

CHAPTER SIX

Going Home

A crowd of elves had gathered with Mrs Christmas and Sarah to say goodbye. 'Bless you, Lambchops!' they called. 'Thank goodness you came! . . . Think if you hadn't! . . . Whew! . . . Farewell, farewell!'

In the Great Sleigh, Sarah's father took up the reins. 'Ready, Lambchops?'

He made a fine appearance now, his hair and beard combed, and wearing a smart green cloak and cap. The famous red suit, he had explained, was reserved for delivering gifts.

'Goodbye, everyone!' called Mrs Lambchop. 'We will remember you always!'

'You bet!' cried Stanley. 'I'll *never* forget!'

46

'But you will, dear,' said Mrs Christmas. 'You will *all* forget.'

'Hardly.' Mr Lambchop smiled. 'An evening like this does not slip one's mind.'

'Poppa will see to it, actually,' said Sarah. 'Snow City, all of us here . . . We're supposed to be, you know, sort of a mystery. Isn't that *silly*? I mean, if—'

'Sarah!' her father said. 'We must go.'

The Lambchops looked up at the night sky, still bright with stars, then turned for a last sight of the little red-roofed house behind them, and of the elves' cottages about the snowy square.

'We are ready,' said Mr Lambchop.

'Goodbye, goodbye!' called Mrs Lambchop and Stanley and Arthur.

'Goodbye, goodbye!' called the elves, waving.

The eight reindeer tossed their heads, jingling their harness bells. One bell flew off, and Stanley caught the little silver cup in his hand. Suddenly, as before, the jingling stopped, all was silence, and the pale mist rose again about the sleigh.

Sarah's father's voice rang clear. 'Come, Dasher, Dancer, Prancer, Vixen! Come, Comet, Cupid, Donder and . . . oh, whatsisname?'

'Blitzen!' Stanley called.
'Thank you. Come, Blitzen!'
The mist swirled, closing upon the sleigh.

CHAPTER SEVEN

Christmas

The Lambchops all remarked the next morning on how soundly they had slept, and how late. Mr Lambchop ate breakfast in a rush.

'Will you be all day at the office, George?' Mrs Lambchop asked. 'It *is* Christmas Eve, you know.'

'There is much to do,' said Mr Lambchop. 'I will be kept late, I'm afraid.'

But there was little to occupy him at his office, since a practical joker had left word he would not be in. He was home by noon to join friends and family for carol singing about the neighbourhood.

Mrs Lambchop had the carolers in for hot

50

chocolate, which was greatly admired. She had added cinnamon, she explained; the idea had just popped into her head. The carolers were all very jolly, and Frank Smith, who lived next door, made everyone laugh, the Lambchops hardest of all, by claiming he had seen reindeer on their lawn the night before.

On Christmas morning, they opened their gifts to each other, and gifts from relatives and friends. Then came a surprise for Stanley and Arthur. Mr Lambchop had just turned on the TV news.

' . . . and now a flash from South America, from where the earthquake was,' the announcer was saying. 'Homeless villagers here are giving thanks this morning for a tremendous supply of socks, shirts, underwear, and food. They have also received a *thousand* tents, and a *thousand* little stoves to cook on!' The screen showed a homeless villager, looking grateful. 'The tents, and the little stoves,' the villager said. 'Just what we need! Bless whoever sends these tents and stoves! Also the many tasty chocolate bars with nuts!'

'He's blessing *me*!' cried Stanley. 'I asked for tents in my letter. But I wasn't sure it would work.'

'Well, *I* wrote about stoves.' Arthur said.

'*And* chocolate bars. But they didn't have to have nuts.'

Happy coincidences! thought Mr and Mrs Lambchop, smiling at each other.

Christmas dinner, shared with various aunts, uncles, and cousins, was an enormous meal of turkey, yams, and three kinds of pie. Then everyone went ice-skating in the park. By bedtime, Stanley and Arthur were more than ready for sleep.

'A fine holiday,' said Mr Lambchop, tucking Arthur in.

'Yes indeed.' Mrs Lambchop tucked in Stanley. 'Pleasant dreams, boys, and – What's this?' She had found something on the table by his bed. 'Why, it's a little bell! A silver bell!'

'It was in my pocket,' Stanley said. 'I don't know what it's from.'

'Pretty. Goodnight, you two,' said Mrs Lambchop, and switched off the light.

The brothers lay silent for a moment in the dark.

'Stanley . . .?' Arthur said. 'It *was* a nice holiday, don't you think.'

'*Extra* nice,' said Stanley. 'But why? It's as if I have something wonderful to remember, but can't think what.'

'Me too. Merry Christmas, Stanley.'

'Merry Christmas, Arthur,' said Stanley, and soon they were both asleep.

THE END

Jeff Brown

FLAT STANLEY

Stanley Lambchop is just a normal healthy boy, though since an enormous noticeboard fell on him while he was asleep he's been only half an inch thick!

Stanley finds he can now squeeze under doors, be lowered down a grating and even be posted in an envelope to California.

A hilarious story, now a classic.

Jeff Brown

STANLEY AND THE MAGIC LAMP

Stanley Lambchop is polishing his Mum's birthday teapot when a boy genie appears out of the spout. The genie starts granting Stanley's wishes right away and the Lambchop family are in for some surprises!

This funny and delightful sequel to Flat Stanley was originally published as *A Lamp for the Lambchops*.

Jeff Brown

STANLEY IN SPACE

This third Lambchop family adventure by the author of *Flat Stanley* is both funny and brilliant.

'Will you meet with us?
Does anyone hear?'

From the great farness of space, the Tyrrans call to Earth.

Who will meet them? And how?

The President of the United States chooses Stanley Lambchop and his family to become the first humans to explore in *Star Scout*, the new top-secret spaceship.

Stanley's most exciting adventure is about to begin . . . Who are the Tyrrans? What do they want?

Patrick Skene-Catling

THE CHOCOLATE TOUCH

John Midas is a normal, average sort of boy – until he finds an old coin in the road. He uses it to buy a very special box of chocolates. It contains the most chocolaty chocolate John Midas has ever eaten – but it leaves him with a gift that could be a dream come true . . . or a nightmare. Everything he touches turns to chocolate!

'A brilliantly told story . . . Highly recommended . . .'

Books for Keeps

'The escalation of alarming happenings is neatly managed and John's change of heart brings a splendid piece of parodic fantasy to a satisfying end.'

Growing Point

'It is told with an engaging humour that boys and girls will instantly discover and approve.'

Saturday Review, USA

W J Corbett

LITTLE ELEPHANT

Tumf (short for Tumffington) is the luckiest little elephant in Africa until the terrible day when the ivory poachers make him an orphan.

Tumf sets out on a nightmarish journey but finds friends along the way, including a veagle (a vulture posing as an eagle?), a tortoise and a cheeky little monkey.

Across Africa, through desert and swamp, water and land, happy and sad, Tumf plods on in his quest for happiness.

A funny and touching story by the author of *The Song of Pentecost*, winner of the Whitbread Award.

'The author has a great capacity for endowing his creations with the fancies and foibles we humans recognise as our own. His animals seem to behave just that bit more responsibly . . .'
Junior Bookshelf

Nicholas Fisk

THE TALKING CAR

'*Boring yourself!*' *said the voice of the car.*
  '*WHAT?*' *said Rob, amazed.*

The voice that had only said 'Fasten your seat belts!' was suddenly answering back. Rob and the car become great friends – but what will happen when Rob's father tries to sell the car?

'A lively, fast-moving, warm and comic book . . .'
Books for Your Children

'this story is original, clever and witty . . . the entire book is a pleasure to read.'
Lance Salway

Andrew Matthews

LOADS OF TROUBLE

'Well, m'lady, the village has got a problem with your . . . er . . .' Councillor Earwacker cast about for words like a man trying to find his slippers in a dark bedroom. At last, inspiration struck him and made his eyes go glittery. 'The village has got a problem with your elephant unmentionables, m'lady!' he announced.

Lady Feeblerick is outraged when her elephants are accused of causing an unsavoury pollution problem. And she is even more outraged when she thinks the elephants will have to go. Will their keeper Toby Hoken and his mysterious assistant Bat be able to save them from certain trouble . . .?

An hilarious tale of adventure from the author of *Wickedoz, Wolf Pie, Mistress Moonwater* and *Dr Monsoon Taggert's Amazing Finishing Academy* which was shortlisted for the 1989 Smarties Prize.

Hazel Townson

CHARLIE THE CHAMPION LIAR

To keep face after a disappointing birthday, Charlie Lyle pretends he's been given a video camera. But he quickly finds that this one small lie draws him into a whole series of lies when someone suggests he makes a video of a PE display . . .

A wonderfully funny story by a master storyteller, whose books have previously been described by Stephanie Nettell as 'rollicking rough and tumble fun'.

'an amusing story with a bit of a moral . . .'
Junior Bookshelf

A Selected List of Fiction from Mammoth

While every effort is made to keep prices low, it is sometimes necessary to increase prices at short notice. Mandarin Paperbacks reserves the right to show new retail prices on covers which may differ from those previously advertised in the text or elsewhere.

The prices shown below were correct at the time of going to press.

☐	7497 1421 2	**Betsey Biggalow is Here!**	Malorie Blackman	£2.99
☐	7497 0366 0	**Dilly the Dinosaur**	Tony Bradman	£2.99
☐	7497 0137 4	**Flat Stanley**	Jeff Brown	£2.99
☐	7497 0568 X	**Dorrie and the Goblin**	Patricia Coombs	£2.50
☐	7497 0983 9	**The Real Tilly Beany**	Annie Dalton	£2.99
☐	7497 0592 2	**The Peacock Garden**	Anita Desai	£2.99
☐	7497 0054 8	**My Naughty Little Sister**	Dorothy Edwards	£2.99
☐	7497 0723 2	**The Little Prince (colour ed.)**	A. Saint-Exupery	£3.99
☐	7497 0305 9	**Bill's New Frock**	Anne Fine	£2.99
☐	7497 1530 8	**Who's a Clever Girl, Then?**	Rose Impey	£2.99
☐	7497 0041 6	**The Quiet Pirate**	Andrew Matthews	£2.99
☐	7497 0420 9	**I Don't Want To!**	Bel Mooney	£2.99
☐	7497 1496 4	**Miss Bianca in the Orient**	Margery Sharp	£2.99
☐	7497 0048 3	**Friends and Brothers**	Dick King Smith	£2.99
☐	7497 0795 X	**Owl Who Was Afraid of the Dark**	Jill Tomlinson	£2.99
☐	7497 0915 4	**Little Red Fox Stories**	Alison Uttley	£2.99

All these books are available at your bookshop or newsagent, or can be ordered direct from the address below. Just tick the titles you want and fill in the form below.

Cash Sales Department, PO Box 5, Rushden, Northants NN10 6YX.
Fax: 0933 410321 : Phone 0933 410511.

Please send cheque, payable to 'Reed Book Services Ltd.', or postal order for purchase price quoted and allow the following for postage and packing:

£1.00 for the first book, 50p for the second; **FREE POSTAGE AND PACKING FOR THREE BOOKS OR MORE PER ORDER.**

NAME (Block letters) ....

ADDRESS ....

....

☐ I enclose my remittance for ....

☐ I wish to pay by Access/Visa Card Number ⬚⬚⬚⬚⬚⬚⬚⬚⬚⬚⬚⬚⬚⬚⬚⬚

Expiry Date ⬚⬚⬚⬚

Signature ....

Please quote our reference: MAND